Antra,

Something to remind you of your Christian service at Ardclanaig and of the appreciation of your friends here.

Best wishes for the future and may you find God's word to be a lamp for your feet and a light to your path. Psalm 119 v 105

Phil Fryson
Centre Director
Abernethy, Ardclanaig
5th April 2010

TALES
OF THE
TAY

Tales
of the
Tay

Joan Pearson

northernbooks
from Famedram

JOAN PEARSON, who wrote *Tales of the Tay* in 1975, was married to the much decorated World War II soldier Brigadier Alastair Pearson. To mark the book's re-issue, and in memory of this much loved couple, the publishers have made a donation to the Tullochan Trust, the charity founded to honour his name.

Also by Joan Pearson:

Loch Lomond: The Maid and the Loch
Kilmartin: The Stones of History

ISBN 0905 489 76 4
© Copyright 2003 Famedram Publishers Ltd AB41 9EA

Contents

Introduction

The Tay rises on Ben Laoigh, at the south-west end of the Grampians. It's the longest river in Scotland – at about 120 miles – and, in a land of beautiful rivers, has no peer; it also produces more cubic feet of water per minute than any other river in the United Kingdom.

The word Tay is derived not from the usual Gaelic of these parts but comes from the even earlier language of the ancient Britons. It was composed, I suppose, of the first sounds ever strung together by man to form a means of communication, when 'a' meant water and 'ta' meant the water or river. Rivers like Taw, Tamar, Tagus, Thames and the Aar in Switzerland, take their names from the same source.

In its infancy, up in Ben Laoigh, or the Ben of the Calves, it starts its long journey to the sea as the *Allt-an-Lund, allt* meaning burn. Soon it becomes the Coninish river, then the Fillan which flows into Loch Dochart. When it emerges it has become and remains the Dochart till it enters Loch Tay at Killin. There, you might say, it comes into its own, for on leaving the loch at Kenmore, it is indeed the Tay, has given up childish things and settled down to the business of life.

From Kenmore it flows in a leisurely fashion to Aberfeldy; the pace quickens between Aberfeldy and Dunkeld, through Strathtay and the most beautiful part of its journey. Then it wanders off eastwards to its assignation with the Isla and eventually lands up in majesty at Perth, which is the end of our, but not the Tay's journey.

The story goes that a certain legionary of Agricola's army on his first sight of the Tay, here at Perth, exclaimed, 'Ecce Tiber' or 'Behold the Tiber.' Presumably meant as a compliment, this opening gambit doesn't appear to have gone down very well with the natives. As Sir Walter Scott put it, most succinctly:

"Behold the Tiber, the vain Roman cried,
Viewing the ample Tay from Bailgie's side;
But where's the Scot that would this vaunt
repay
And hail the puny Tiber for the Tay?"

Loch Tay is reputed to be the actual centre of Scotland and for a very great number of years the loch and its river were at the very heart of Scottish life, The Tay has seen history in the making; it has carried the hollowed out tree-trunk canoes of primitive man, the coracles, Roman galleys and the Viking longships which reached Dunkeld. On many occasions it must have run red with the blood of Pict and Scot, Roman and Caledonian, Viking and Dane, ancestors.

Dunkeld, on the banks of the Tay, became the spiritual centre of Scotland. Scone and Perth became the centre of political life. Perth was also an important port. Trade was brisk between Scotland and the west European states. In fact the Tay was Scotland's main artery for nearly 1500 years.

It wasn't till the late 15th century that Perth gradually ceded her position to Edinburgh, which became the capital city – Perth still ranks second to Edinburgh among the cities of Scotland.

In the late 18th and early 19th centuries the Clyde became Scotland's life line and Glasgow and her river took on the unenviable task of becoming Scotland's industrial heart. Perth and the Tay settled down to a long expectation of peaceful days. Which all worked out for the best in the long run, because that strip of desert land between Glasgow and Edinburgh is the only part of this lovely land of ours that is most un-lovely, so by all means 'Let Glasgow Flourish' and leave Tayside to its dreams of yesterday.

Strathfillan

N ow let's go back to the beginning,
to the corrie on Ben Laoigh where
the Tay first sees the light of day. It
is almost smothered at birth with the loveliest
Alpine mosses and tiny flowers of starry
white saxifrage and crimson campion. As it
tumbles down the hillside it is joined by
numerous streams till it reaches the valley of
Strathfillan, east of Tyndrum, where King
Robert the Bruce so nearly met his death at
the hands of MacDougall of Lorne at the
Battle of Dalry, or *Dail-Righ*, the 'Field of the
King'.

Bruce and a small band of followers
were resting here among the mountains after
their defeat at Methven. When news reached
MacDougall, whose father-in-law, the Red
Comyn, Bruce had killed, MacDougall came
with a large band of men to revenge the
Comyn's death. Bruce was greatly out-num-

bered and decided to retreat, fighting a brave rearguard action himself to allow his men time to escape. It was during this skirmish that one of Lorne's men caught hold of his plaid and tried to pull him backwards off his horse.

Luckily for Bruce both plaid and brooch came away in the man's hand. This was, of course, the famous Brooch of Lorne and is now the treasured possession of the MacDougalls of Lorne. It was shown to Queen Victoria when she visited Tayside in 1842. Captain MacDougall was wearing it when he commanded the barge in which the Queen sailed down Loch Tay and she notes in her journal: "Captain Macdougall showed us the real Brooch of Lorne which was taken by his ancestor from Robert Bruce."

St. Fillan, after whom the glen was called, came from Ireland with St. Colomba, St. Adamnan and many other holy Irishmen. Once they'd settled on Iona, in the sixth century, these early missionaries crossed over into Perthshire and set about their Herculean task of spreading the gospel to the 'tribes of Tay.' St. Adamnan's portion was Glen Lyon and Dull. St. Fillan was given Glen Dochart and what later became Strathfillan.

Many burns come cascading down the mountain-sides here in Strathfillan and help to swell the Fillan Water in which, just where a large rock juts over the river, men gathered on one side and women on the other. This was St. Fillan's healing pool, specially beneficial to the insane. These poor witless ones had to immerse themselves in this pool, as above, bring up three stones from the bottom and place them on three different cairns; this operation had to be repeated three times. They were then tied down on the stone floor of the nearby chapel for the night, without any covering. One can imagine if they weren't dead by morning, the shock may well have effected a 'miraculous' cure!

It was King Robert who built the first chapel to St. Fillan's memory, at Kirkton in Strathfillan. Later it became a priory, and you can see the ruins to this day. Two of the Saint's more famous relics, his crozier, or staff. and his bell, are now preserved for posterity in the National Museum of Antiquities in Edinburgh. But after his death his relics were given, for safe keeping, to different lay families in the district and passed down from father to son.

At the Reformation this office of dewar, or caretaker, lapsed. The bell lay on a tombstone in the churchyard of the priory and was used in the rites of curing the insane. Then it was locked up to prevent this use but public outcry caused it to be returned to its wonted place.

In 1798 an English tourist, while staying at the inn at Tyndrum, heard of this famous bell and removed it to his home in Hertfordshire, where it remained for a hundred years. Eventually though it was returned by a descendant. The crozier reached Canada on one of its journeys, but it too finally came home to rest. It is really something of a miracle that these relics should have survived the centuries.

Past Crianlarich is Loch Dochart. There was once a MacDougall stronghold on the island here. One winter night when the loch was frozen, the Macgregors stormed the walls which lie in ruins still. Later it was acquired by the Campbells of Glenorchy. On the north shore of Loch Dochart, where cliffs overhang the deep waters, there is a cave from which resounds an incredible echo. In coaching days the driver used to stop and give his passengers a demonstration with his posthorn of these remarkable reverberations.

A little farther down the glen is the village of Suie, the Gaelic for seat. Here was the very stone on which St. Fillan sat and taught the people the ways of his God. These Irish saints seem to have enjoyed their comforts, for their stone seats abound in Tayside – no peripatetic Aristotelian nonsense for them!

The Wordsworths stayed at the inn during their tour of the Highlands. They enjoyed the scenery but not the food, prices, or the manners of their hosts.

Presently, past Luib, the Dochart makes its spectacular entry into Killin, which lies between two rivers, the gentle Lochay and the turbulent Dochart. The name Killin is derived from the Gaelic, Kill-Phinn. This was the cell or burying place of Fingal, a famous Celtic warrior of the third century. There is a standing stone west of the church, said to be his last resting place.

I don't think there's another town in Scotland that has such a beautiful approach. So many artists, famous and otherwise, have tried to capture the glory of the Falls of Dochart, roaring and thundering over their rocky bed, but no picture can do it justice, you must see it for yourself.

On the right side of the bridge leading into Killin there's an iron gateway, hardly noticeable, and a path that leads you between two stone pillars to an archway, the centre one of three. A little farther on there's a walled enclosure, and here lie the chiefs of the Clan Macnab, while outside are buried other members of the clan.

This famous graveyard is on the island of Inch Buie, or the yellow island, so called because of its carpet of thick yellow moss. The islet lies snuggly between two arms of the Dochart. The day I went to visit it was late spring; the air was full of the heady scent of azaleas, the trees were in their spring finery and the sound of running water was everywhere. Truth to tell I'd be well content to rest my own bones among such beauty.

Indeed one chieftain, Francis Macnab, when proposing marriage to a certain young lady, stressed the fact that he owned the most beautiful burial ground in Scotland. Evidently this proved insufficient inducement, for Francis Macnab was never married – though he is reputed to have fathered 32 children!

A very strange thing happened once on Inch Buie. During a bad storm at the beginning of the last century a branch was torn off a fir tree and fell into the fork of another, where it remained. Gradually, to everyone's amazement, it began to grow, and flourished on its foster parent. This was reckoned by botanists to be an impossibility, the nature of a fir tree being repellent to all extraneous growths, and yet, centuries earlier, this very event had been foretold by the celebrated Lady of Lawers. Her prophecy was that the remaining Macnab lands would be added to the estate of the First Marquis of

Breadalbane, a descendant of the Campbells of Glenorchy. And sure enough, it was just about at the time the fostered fir flourished that the last of the Macnab lands were bought by the Breadalbanes.

The name Macnab has evolved from the Gaelic – Mac-an-Aba, or the son of the abbot. This etymology greatly disturbed one John Macnab in the 18th century.

He feared his ancestors might be considered bastards if this derivation was accepted, because "noe abbot or kirkman in orders befor the reformation were allowed marriage by their canons," as he says in a letter to his brother. Some say the said abbot was a lay one, which sounds a contradiction in terms, but maybe there were such persons.

For nearly a thousand years Glen Dochart was the home of the Macnabs, but, like so many other famous clans of this district, they gradually lost their lands, thanks to the acquisitive habits of comparative newcomers to the district, in this case the Campbells of Glenorchy, whose original patrimony lay to the west. These lairds of Glen Orchy became Earls and Marquises of Breadalbane and finally owned the entire countryside from Aberfeldy to Oban.

Breadalbane means the upland of Alban, Alban was the ancient name for Scotland, and 'braghaid', often found as 'braid' means the 'upper part.'

The boundaries of Breadalbane have never been defined but are roughly that beautiful stretch of land between Tyndrum and the junction of the rivers Tay and Lyon. The original home of the Macnabs was Ellanryne Castle, which was burnt down by the Campbells and Cromwell's men. They then moved to Kinnell House, opposite Killin on the south side of Loch Tay.

The Macnab crest displays the head of a man with a great bushy beard and the motto, 'Timor Omnis Abesto' – Let fear be far from all, or could be translated simply as Fear Naught. They certainly lived up to their motto.

The Clans of Macnish and Macnab were at perpetual war with each other and once, at Christmas time, things came to a head, so to speak. The Macnabs had sent a henchman to Crieff for provisions for the feast. He was waylaid and robbed on his way home by Macnish's men.

This was too much. Finlay, the Macnab chieftain, addressed his twelve stalwart but hungry sons: "The night is the night, if the lads were the lads." The challenge was taken up with alacrity, and the twelve collected their boat, carried it on their shoulders over the mountain tracks to Loch Earn, and rowed across to the island on which the Macnishes had their stronghold. They found them celebrating with their ill-gotten goods – not really in the mood for battle. With one mighty blow Smooth John, the eldest of the Macnab's sons, decapitated the bushy, bearded head of the Macnish and the remaining members of the Clan were slaughtered.

The chieftain's head was born proudly home to show the Macnab that his suggestion had been well and truly executed. Hence the crest and motto. In the early 19th century the 17th Laird of Macnab emigrated to Canada, having been left an enormous load of debt by his uncle, the famous Francis. The family lands were sold – mainly to the Campbells of Glenorchy – as the Lady of Lawers had prophesied.

But the Macnab story has a happy ending. For a hundred years or more the chieftainship lay dormant and the Campbells flourished. By the beginning of the 20th century, however, eventually their fortunes waned and they, in turn, had to sell their possessions. The 9th Earl of Breadalbane sold back Kinnell House and 7000 acres to Archibald Macnab, a member of a cadet branch of the clan, who had been declared

by Lyon Court to be the 22nd Chief and
Macnab of Macnab. And so, at last, the
Macnabs returned to the land of their fathers.

There is now a tweed mill on your left
after crossing the Bridge of Dochart. But long
ago this was the site of St. Fillan's flour mill.
Nearby there was an enormous ash tree,
under which there used to be another of the
Saint's stone seats. A great storm in 1856
washed it away and it was never seen again.
Here too, the Saint kept his eight healing
stones, each faintly resembling the portion of
the anatomy they were meant to cure.

About a mile from Killin, across the
Lochay, are the ruins of Finlarig Castle.
Finlarig means the white or holy pass,
though there was certainly nothing holy
about it during the Campbell's time. It was
acquired by Sir Duncan Campbell, second
Laird of Glenorchy at the beginning of the
16th century. The castle stands on a mound.
Beside it there is the site of an earlier fort.
From very early days this important pass was
guarded. It was rectangular in shape and four
storeys high: the only entrance left intact is
on the south side and on the lintel above the
door are the Royal Arms and the initials,

IR
AR
1609

These refer to James VI of Scotland and I of England and his Queen, Anne of Denmark: they must have been on calling terms with the Campbell lairds of Glenorchy. The third laird built the chapel at Finlarig "to be ane burial for himself and his posteritie." He obviously felt by that time the Campbells had obtained a sure footing in Breadalbane. The later, grandiose mausoleum, in which 14 chiefs were buried, was built on the same site.

Close by the castle was the beheading pit with its block; an underground passage led from the Castle to this gruesome spot. Beheading was reserved for the upper crust. Hanging was the lot of the common folk – in this case from the branch of a huge oak tree. When cut down some years ago the bough was nearly severed by the rope-worn groove.

And so that the laird's guests might watch the grisly performance in comfort, terraces were built on the site. Imprisonment was not popular – a convicted man was "instantly hangit." They must have had strong stomachs in those days. It was during the times of Grey Colin, the sixth Laird, and his son, Black Duncan, both of whom had the most unsavoury reputations, that Finlarig saw its worst atrocities against mankind.

When a child, Grey Colin was fostered

with the Macgregors of Stronfearnan, now Feranan. This was a complicated arrangement whereby a nobleman's child was farmed out to a family of lower rank. Some cattle were presented to the child by his father. The foster parents gave him the same number and grazed this small herd, which eventually belonged to the child. At the death of the foster parents part of their estate belonged to the child. In return for this the real parents undertook to protect the foster ones. All of which presumably helped to strengthen the family ties of the clan system and was the custom for hundreds of years.

Not in Grey Colin's case however. Two years after he became laird he turned Gregor Dougalson, a kinsman of his foster parents, out of Balloch – near Kenmore – because he wanted to build a castle there. When asked why he was building his latest castle on the eastern extremity of his vast domain, his reply was simple, "We maun just birze ayont," or, drive on regardless, which should have been their motto.

On an earlier occasion he invited the chief of the Macgregor clan and his two sons to be his guest at Finlarig. During the evening's entertainment all three were dragged off to the pit and beheaded.

It was a strange thing, this terrible

hatred of the Campbells for the MacGregors. Caused by jealousy, perhaps of the newcomers towards those who had, for generations, been the much loved and respected lairds of Breadalbane. On several occasions Queen Mary herself intervened on behalf of the Macgregors, but after her imprisonment the feud went on relentlessly – for three hundred years or more.

But if Grey Colin had been bad, Black Duncan was worse. Black Duncan of the Cowl and the Castles, as he was known, on account of his passion for building new, or furbishing up old ones. He was, perhaps the greatest of all the Glenorchy Campbells for acquiring other people's lands, by fair means or foul, though mainly the latter.

He took them from the Menzies, the Robertsons and the Drummonds, but most of all he took from the Macgregors.

"Glenorchy's proud mountain,
Colchurn and her towers,
Glenstrae and Glenlyon no longer are ours,"
was their sad cry.

One saving grace, however, Black Duncan did possess – he was a lover of trees, and it was largely this great love of his, most ably assisted by the climatic conditions of Tayside, that gave future generations some of the loveliest wooded scenery in Scotland. He ordered his tenants to plant saplings of oak, ash, plane and sycamore, to be supplied by his own gardeners at "twa pennies the piece." He also made sure they grew by imposing fines on anyone who dared to damage them, and who would, with that pit so handy?

He it was who planted the stately avenue of limes known as 'the Cathedral' that led to Finlarig – not to mention all the other great trees nearby. There's a sycamore said to be 800 years old, another 600; and across the Loch at Auchmore, again in Campbell country, there are many, many more. Queen Victoria planted a Sequoia Wellingtonia on her historic visit to the Marquis in 1842 and it has already achieved vast proportions.

Auchmore, a little south-east of Kinnell, was rebuilt by the ninth Earl in a somewhat inappropriate Italian style – he retired there after being forced to sell the larger portion of his vast estates. But in the end even Auchmore had to go, and was eventually taken over by the North of Scotland Hydro Electric Board. Sic transit gloria mundi, and no mistake.

Finlarig comes into the news again in 1645 when the Marquis of Montrose, with his rabble army of Irishmen and Highlanders, made his whirlwind attack down Tayside. Plundering and burning, they made their way to join battle with the Duke of Argyll, who, with the Campbells of Glenorchy, were supporting the Covenanters. Sir Robert, the ninth Laird, had placed garrisons in all his strongholds in Tayside, even in the hitherto abandoned little Isle of Lochtay.

Finlarig however seems to have escaped any great damage on this occasion. Ten years later it was occupied by Monk's men, when he became Governor of Scotland in Cromwell's time.

In 1745 Finlarig was garrisoned by the Argyllshire militia, as were Kilchurn and Kingshouse, thus holding all the passes on the west against the Jacobites. Today trees are growing from Finlarig's ruined walls

Now let's pay a visit to Ardeonaig, on the south side of the loch. The old road from Killin to Kenmore was on this side. The present and more frequented one to the north was built by the Earl of Breadalbane in the 18th century. This was said to be "a most excellent road," with 32 stone bridges crossing the mountain burns. But the old road is much more beautiful. It has trees and lovely cascading streams, and between the trees you can see the beauty and majesty of Ben Lawers, keeping watch over its loch.

All that is left of the old pre-reformation church lies on the hillside above the farm of

Dall. The old font has been placed in the graveyard and there's a delightful 400 year old inn known as Tigh-na-Linnhe, or the house of the pool.

The minister of Ardeonaig at one time also had charge of Lawers, across the loch. It must have been arduous, even for a good oarsman. In 1791 he was receiving the princely emolument of £50 per annum. The schoolmaster had £15, "for his encouragement."

According to the Society for the Promotion of Christian Knowledge, Ardeonaig needed an itinerant school, and in Edinburgh on November 16th, 1731 they presented Duncan Wright, ingoing schoolmaster, with fourteen books of a religious nature, mainly Bibles, a few copy books and some writing paper and sent him off on his 90 miles walk to Ardeonaig, where he proved a very successful dominie. In Ardtalnaig, the next village, Patrick Forbes, "who taught a school and was poor," was given three shillings for three ells of cloth. There's nothing new under the sun – not even social security.

In far off days, when people could see a little further than their noses, Tayside was famed for its Urisks, or little people. The word Urisk comes from the Gaelic for water, 'uisge,' which sounds something like whisky. That's after all how whisky got its name, 'uisge-baugh', which means, literally, the water of life. The haunts of these Urisks were pools, waterfalls, and moorland lochs. They were rather like robins in that they kept to their own beats. They could be very mischievous if tormented but where they were appreciated would do all kinds of useful jobs about the place.

As we re-cross the loch on our way to Lawers, the Carwhin Burn enters it and there's a pleasing little story told of a young Urisk whose haunts were thereabouts. He was forever annoying a certain farmer's wife by asking her name. Over and over again he would ask and she kept replying, "I am myself, nobody but myself." Still he kept on with his questions till at last, in a rage, she threw a pan of hot water over his bare legs. When the Urisk's father, Sligeachan, heard the awful noise his son was making he came to investigate and asked his son who had done this thing. The reply was, "myself, nobody but myself," and that's how the good wife of Carwhin got rid of her annoying Urisk and Sligeachan never knew the truth of it.

The lands of Lawers were one of the earliest possessions on Loch Tayside of the Glenorchy Campbells. They were bestowed on Sir Colin, the First Laird by James III for helping to capture the murderers of his grandfather James I. Their original home was thought to have been close to the loch shore, west of the Lawers Burn. This was destroyed during Montrose's raid in 1645, and the ruins of a two storeyed house on the same spot would be those of their second home. This was where the Lady of Lawers came to live when she married a younger brother of the sixth laird in the middle of the 17th century.

Many of the Lady's prophecies were connected with the old church of Lawers, now a ruin, the building of which, by the sixth laird, she must have watched with interest. She said that a tree would grow near the church and when it reached the height of the gables the Church of Scotland would be rent in twain.

Sure enough, this stage of its development coincided with the Disruption of the Church in 1843. When the tree reached the ridge of the church the House of Breadalbane would be without an heir and this happened in 1862, with the death of the second Marquis. She also said that whoever cut the tree down would come to an evil end. The rash farmer who ventured to prove the Lady wrong was gored to death by his bull, his accomplice lost his wits and even the horse which assisted in this venture came to a sudden and untimely end.

War memorial, Killin

Falls of Dochart and Ben Lawers

Falls of Dochart, Killin

Clan Macnab burial ground, Killin

Parish church, Killin

Main street, Killin

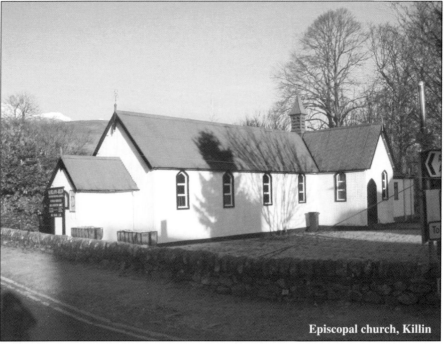

Episcopal church, Killin

Bridge of Lochay Hotel

Bridge of Lochay

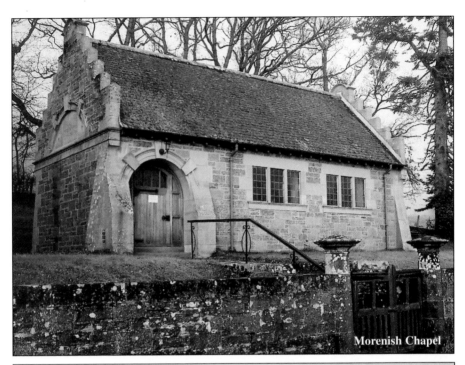

Morenish Chapel

Horn carver, Lawers Toll

The disused Carie Church, formerly operated as a mission church from Kenmore.

Ben Lawers and its information centre

One man and his dog: John Angus Macleod, Lawers shepherd

She foresaw a period when the lands of Lochtayside would be intensively cultivated with a meal mill on every stream, a plough in every lad's hand and both sides of the loch would be like a kail garden. About the end of the 18th century all this did happen; there were two hundred ploughs on the south side and fourteen meal mills on both. But beyond this time of well-being she said the day would come "when the district would first be riddled and then sifted of its people."

This happened with the cruel evictions of the second Marquis, as it did all over Scotland. Small holdings were joined together to make large sheep runs, "the jaw of the sheep would drive the plough out of the ground," as the Lady of Lawers put it. The walls of the little houses were knocked down, the thatched roofs pulled off and burnt and the people had nowhere to lay their heads, in fact the homesteads became so distant from each other "that the one cock would not be able to hear its neighbour crow."

She also foresaw the break up of the Breadalbane estates. Each successive laird, from Colin, the first, to the First Marquis had only one aim in life, "to conquer and to keep thingis conquest," until their lands stretched for a hundred miles across Scotland. The fall of this empire began in 1922 and is now complete

All in all, she was a remarkable lady, and she lies buried beside the old church of which she made so many prophecies. And all the while Ben Lawers, almost 4000 feet of him, looks down in pity, almost, at the junketings of man. The National Trust for Scotland has him in its safe keeping.

The rock of which the Ben is mainly formed is, I'm told, metamorphic schist, which weathers down to a very friable tilth, with even some traces of lime – almost un-heard of in our Scottish hills. This is the reason why it has become a botanist's para-dise, and indeed, the richest source of Alpine flowers in the British Isles. What is more exciting is that Arctic plants have survived here since the last Ice Age, which melted away from Scotland 11,000 years ago.

One of the rarest flowers that flourishes on Ben Lawers is the saxifrage cernia, the drooping saxifrage, found nowhere else in Britain. One of the loveliest is the mountain forget-me-not, *myosotis alpestrie,* which covers the precipitous crags on the west of the Ben with garlands of turquoise blue.

The best of a mountain garden is that its season lasts for so long. Once the flowers on the lower slopes are over and done, all you have to do is climb a little higher when you will find them in full glory all over again, and so on till the summit is reached and the sky takes over from the forget-me-nots.

In a corrie to the west of the Cane Burn, up the old track that was used to carry down the peats, are the remains of the old summer shielings of the district. These shielings were where the women brought their cattle to graze the mountain pastures from June to September, when they were needed at home to bring in the harvest. The huts they lived in were made of stones found lying on the ground, roofed with branches and sods and when the weather was bad can hardly have provided shelter from the elements.

These girls passed their days in watching their little dun coloured cows grazing, milking them and making butter and cheese to last through the winter. And when they were doing none of these things they were spinning wool to clothe their families. There always had to be a burn near the shieling, not only for drinking but also for washing the milk dishes and making butter. And I'm sure they were not entirely bereft of male company, these maidens of the shielings, for surely, when their day's work was done, the young men from the farms would be paying them a visit and having a ceilidh now and then.

The Gaelic word for Lawers means 'the noisy or sounding one' and refers to the burn of that name nearby, which makes a very loud noise when in spate, and from which both the village and Ben take their name.

In another burn that comes from the mountain lochan known as Lochan-nan-Cat, there is a waterfall, behind which is a cave. Once a Macgregor sheltered here when chased by an Italian bloodhound and some Campbells. The old story goes that one particular litter of this breed of dogs was suckled by a Macgregor woman so that they would be better able to follow and track down Macgregors.

In this case the pursuers could find no trace of their prey and abandoned the search. Not so the bloodhound, who kept sniffing about the heather where the Macgregor had entered the water. An arrow from his bow however soon put an end to the hound, said to be the last of that litter.

Ardtalnaig and Acharn

Let's go down the mountain now to the Loch shore and pretend we're going to be ferried across to Ardtalnaig, as we would have been in days gone by. But just before we do so, where the Lawers Burn enters the loch, are the remains of old lint mills, the first ever to be built in the Highlands, by that humble genius, Hugh Cameron, who was born in Lawers and worked there as a mill-wright.

He was the first man ever to introduce spinning wheels into Breadalbane. He made hundreds and showed the people how to use them. He also persuaded them to grow flax and up in the shielings the women became thread manufacturers and people came from far and wide to Kenmore market to buy this thread from the hills.

And what of Hugh Cameron? He lived

for one hundred and twelve years and must have died well satisfied with his life's work.

Ardtalnaig, or the high pass, was once an important place on Lochtay. It guarded the pass from the south, from Comrie, Crieff, Stirling and Perth to the north. There is still a path over the hills from Comrie.

The early kings of Scotland had a hunting lodge here, the Castle of Tay, on the present site of Milton farm, probably built by Malcolm 1004-1034. They were certainly frequent visitors to Tayside, for the fishing, and shooting. The loch must have been as famous for salmon then as it is now. Donald IV was drowned here in 647 and the ancient forests of Mamlorn and Ben More must have provided great and varied sport for the guns. Wolves were frequent and unwanted visitors even as late as the 17th century. There's an old Litany of Dunkeld that contains the following prayer: "From caterans and robbers, from wolves and all wild beasts, good Lord deliver us."

East of Ardtalnaig is Acharn, the field of the cairn. It was built at the end of the 18th century by the fourth Earl and first Marquis of Breadalbane to improve the conditions of his people. His tenants were given free grazing for two cows, work on the Taymouth estates and a meal mill. This was in an effort to persuade his Highlanders to settle down to a decent, steady life. In those days, industry, to a Highlander, was a dirty word. He much preferred to fight and steal another man's cattle for a livelihood. An industrious man was looked down upon. But very gradually things changed, thanks largely to the efforts of the third and fourth Earls of Breadalbane.

At the time of writing, Acharn is a busy little place; the old mill has been renovated by a craftsman who specialises in the reproduction of Highland weapons in leather and wood and exports them in large quantities to America. The lovely Celtic designs of the Kenmore church pew tapestries, made up by the ladies – and gentlemen – of the parish, were also his doing. There's an engineering business here too that makes wonderful winches used by lumberjacks the world over.

But the most beautiful thing in Acharn is its Falls. Though they don't possess the grandeur of the Falls of Moness at Aberfeldy, in a miniature form they are just as beautiful.

Now let's wend our way back to the ferry-that-used-to-be and cross the Loch to Fearnan – the place of alders. These Fearnan lands belonged to the Robertsons until the ubiquitous Campbells took over. One of these Robertsons, Alexander, the Chief of his clan and a staunch Jacobite, seems to have been a likeable and irascible character, a soldier and a poet. He was with the exiled King James in France, fought in the '15 rebellion and was taken prisoner at Sheriffmuir. He escaped, but was too old to take an active part in the '45, and died in 1749.

There is a letter in the records of Kenmore Parish Church addressed to the Rev. John Hamilton, written in 1730. Some of the chief's tenants had evidently complained that seats allocated to them in Kenmore church were being usurped by others, forcing them to stand during the service. You must bear in mind the Rev. John was a staunch Hanoverian – the letter goes like this:-

"Sir, Since my tenants, I do not know by what inspiration, are willing to hear a person of your persuasion, I hope you will not see them dispossessed.

"Their seats in the kirk are well known, pray let them sit easy and have elbow room... You, who are a kind of exorcist, cast out the spirit of oppression, hatred and malice from amongst us, that every man may possess his Paternal inheritance, from the Throne in Westminster Abbay to the cobbler's sate in the Kirk of Kenmore."

Great stuff.

Glen Lyon

N ow let's diverge a little from the story of the Tay, let's turn left up the hill at Fearnan and take the road to Glen Lyon, for the Lyon is one of Tay's main tributaries. It is also very beautiful, the longest and narrowest glen in Scotland. In olden times drovers took its mountain tracks to trysts at Achallader and Oban. But today it leads nowhere. I think, because of this passers-by are inclined to pass it by – little do they know what they're missing.

The first time I saw Glen Lyon was in late spring; one of those gold and white days, gold with the blossoms of broom and whin, white with Queen Anne's lace and hawthorn. Even the air was filled with gold and white petals tossed about by the breeze and the shadows were dark and deep. The glen enjoys a pervading sense of peace that cocoons you from the outside world and its troubles.

It's as though the gentle spirit of St. Adamnan, or Eonan as he was known locally, still hovers about his old haunts, for Glen Lyon was very much his glen. Here he built his cell, at Milton Eonan, here he set up his corn mill for the people and here he stayed the plague – the spot is marked by a stone cross. He achieved this 'miracle' by the sensible method of isolating the sick and sending the healthy up into the mountains.

Three centuries before Adamnan came to Glen Lyon it sheltered Fingal, the famous Celtic warrior chief, and his followers, the Fingalians. Fortunately he had a son, Ossian, a bard of great repute, who recounted the mighty deeds of his great father, so that his name and fame have lived on.

Ossian said:– "Twelve castles had Fionn, in the dark bent glen of the stones," and there are the remains of five left – four at Cashlie. The Gaelic word for the glen means the 'bent glen of the stones', presumably on account of these round stone forts or 'duns'. They were used for shelter and protection and also for passing news of impending trouble quickly down the glen.

Each tower was visible to its neighbour and burning flares perhaps were used as signals. There was another of these 'duns' on Drummond Hill, to the east, which connected those in the glen with a line of forts that protected the Pictish border from Finlarig to Stonehaven on the North Sea

The entrance to this peaceful glen is by the Pass of Lyon, where the river has had to force its way through a deep, rocky ravine. The grandeur of it takes your breath away. Far below road level the river rushes and swirls in deep, dark torrents over its rocky bed. If you look down over the wall it almost makes you dizzy and overhead and all around are those lovely great trees, shutting you in and the sky out.

This was where a Macgregor, the heir to the chieftainship, made his famous leap when escaping from his in-laws and their bloodhounds. (He'd been visiting his Campbell wife at Carnban, the home of Red Duncan of the Hospitality, farther down the glen.)

There's a prominent rock jutting over the river on the opposite side that makes this feat just humanly possible. Though he escaped on this occasion he was captured later. He was imprisoned at Balloch Castle and executed on Kenmore Green after a mock trial for trying to stop the Campbells of Glenorchy from taking his lawful heritage.

His poor wife watched the execution and poured out her woe in a pitiful lullaby to her infant son.

> *"Ochain, ochain, ochain, darling,*
> *Sad at heart am I,*
> *Ochain, ochain, ochain, darling,*
> *Thy dad hears not our cry.*
> *On oaken block they laid his head*
> *And made his blood to flow;*
> *Had I a cup to hold it, I'd sup of it I*
>   *know.*
> *Oh! that Finlarig were burning*
> *And Balloch lying low...."*

And both her wishes came true, in time.

Chesthill

B ack on the glen road is Chesthill House; rumour has it that it was from here, or Meggernie Castle, farther down the glen, that Captain Robert Campbell of Glen Lyon, whose niece was married to the MacDonald chieftain's son, set forth on his journey to Glencoe and the terrible massacre at that journey's end.

His contemporaries could understand and forgive the rage that Robert Campbell felt against the MacDonalds, who had, on numerous occasions stolen his cattle and slain his dependants. On one raid alone they 'lifted' 36 horses, 240 cows, 993 sheep and 133 goats – the entire stock in fact, valued at £7540, none of which was ever recovered.

No, it was not so much the savagery of it, for these were fearsome times, it was the treachery that was so unforgivable. Robert Campbell had been a guest of the Mac-

Donalds for a fortnight; every day he'd had his 'morning' with the chief or one of his sons – this was a draught of raw *usquebaugh* (whisky) and he'd accepted an invitation to dine with the chief the evening after the massacre was planned.

> *"For he smiled as a friend, as he*
> *planned as a foe,*
> *To redden each hearthstone in misty*
> *Glencoe."*

Thanks to a snowstorm that delayed reinforcements from Fort William, the carnage was not complete and some did escape, including the two sons of the chief, though Captain Campbell's instructions were to make sure that neither the fox nor his cubs escaped.

The Massacre of Glencoe does not come within our bounds, but the doings of the Earls of Breadalbane certainly do and the first Earl was deeply involved in the whole horrible episode. It was said of him that he was "cunning as a fox, wise as a serpent, but slippery as an eel," – that he cared for no government and no religion unless it suited his own purpose to do so, in fact. "In Edinburgh he was Willie's man and in the Highlands he was Jamie's."

Anyway, he was given £12000 – a lot of
money then – to bribe the Highland chiefs to
swear allegiance to William and Mary and
forswear the Stewarts. The story goes that the
Highlanders never saw a penny of this and
on later questioning the Earl said that the
money had been spent, the Highlands were
quiet, and that was that. After the carnage
on that February day in 1692, there was such
an uproar throughout the country that a
public enquiry was held. Though the Earl of
Breadalbane was not charged with complicity
in the affair, which must have needed all his
slipperiness and cunning, he was charged
with treason, on account of statements made
by him during his negotiations with the chiefs
in 1691. He was imprisoned in Edinburgh for
a short time but was released, on King
William's instructions, without any proceed-
ings being taken.

Across the river from Chesthill there's a
very ancient and attractive little bridge, said
to be Roman, that spans the Allt-Dà-Ghob as
it enters the Lyon. No road passes that way
now, but in olden days the river followed a
different course. It ran north of the so-called
Roman Camp in Fortingall, not south as it
does now, so the road, or track, would then
have followed the south bank of the Lyon. It
was most likely one of the old drove roads,

which might, of course, have followed an earlier, possibly Roman road.

Past Milton Eonan and Bridge of Balgie comes Meggernie, a very pleasing white-washed castle built by Mad Colin Campbell in the 16th century. It contains, or did, a dungeon with iron chains and a hook, from which miscreants were suspended by the middle rib, among other charming forms of medieval torture.

During the 18th century that other great lover of trees, Sir James Menzies of Culdarees and Meggernie, planted them all through Glen Lyon. His are the arboreal milestones from Meggernie to Fortingall; one beech tree at one mile from Meggernie, two at two miles and so on, till the grand total of eleven was reached at Fortingall. He also introduced the first larches into Scotland, from seed he brought back from the Tyrol.

It was either here or at Castle Menzies that he planted them in his greenhouse, where they wilted, were thrown on the compost heap and given up for lost. However, they approved of their new site, flourished, and have done so ever since.

Fortingall

The glen road leads you on into the high hills but it's time to return to the every-day world and Fortingall. This is a fascinating little place and the legend that has come down to us so determinedly through all the intervening years is that Pontius Pilate was born here. It's such an unlikely tale for anyone to have invented, nobody in their wildest dreams would have thought of it, so perhaps it's true, and this is how it all came about.

In the time of Queen Elizabeth I there was an historian called Holinshed from whose work Shakespeare took many of his plots. According to Holinshed, some few years before the birth of Christ, the Emperor Augustus sent emissaries to the Picts, as he did to all other peoples in the then known world, with the aim of achieving universal peace. "His ambassadors went also unto King Metellanus, the King of the Scottishmen," Holinshed says. These envoys were received by Metellanus at Dun-Gael, a fort on the hill behind Fortingall, while the Roman contingent, some of whom had brought their wives, camped in the vale below, and among them was one called Pilate.

They brought rich gifts to the King and a peace pact was eventually signed, followed by many celebrations. They then spent the winter at Fortingall and here Pilate's son was born and they called him Pontius. The Gaelic word for Fortingall is *Feart-nan Gael*, the strong place of the strangers. Perhaps the strangers were the Romans and perhaps the Roman camp on the low ground between the present village and the river, always bravely marked as such on Ordnance Survey maps, and always hotly disputed – perhaps it really was a Roman camp. Just a little one.

One reason against the Roman version is that it is sited in a very vulnerable position with nothing between the camp and the wild mountain passes to the north, which the Romans knew were "rough, wet, wooded and horrid." However, if as seems likely, the Lyon has changed course, in Roman times it would have cut across the low lying isthmus where Fortingall now stands to the Pass of Lyon.

The camp would have been south of the river from which it would have received some protection, instead of having it at its back, as is now the case, where it would certainly have been a great disadvantage. Some say it could well have been the head-quarters of a temporary military station, in which case the troops might have encamped in tents outside the praetorium, which could have occupied the site of the present mound.

Any signs of lighter defences, such as ditches and earthworks, would have been obliterated when the Lyon changed its course. If this *was* a Roman camp it would have been built either in the time of Agricola, 82 A.D., or Severus, in 209 A.D. The site has, as yet, never been 'dug'.

The famous Fortingall yew stands, or is propped up, in the churchyard, and is by now rather a pathetic sight – in fact there's not much of it to be seen. It is surrounded by iron railings and its ancient limbs, which are falling apart, are supported by concrete pillars. Even I, who love old things, think it's time it had an honourable burial.

Pennant, that intrepid traveller of the eighteenth century, says that the trunk was 56 feet in circumference in his day. But it is now sadly mutilated. Nevertheless it is reckoned to be the oldest bit of vegetation in

Europe – 3000 years or more. It would have been an old tree in the days of Metellanus and a sapling when Nebuchadnezzar was King of the Jews.

Sir James Macgregor, the famous Dean of Lismore, who produced the collection of Gaelic poetry known as The Book of the Dean of Lismore, was vicar of Fortingall early in the 16th century. He also originated the Chronicle of Fortingall, which was continued by his successor all through the Reformation. Written in a quaint mixture of Latin and English, it makes very good reading, with many caustic and apt descriptions of the departed, such as, "James Campbell of Lawers... pray for his soul, he broke all his bones on the stair of the inn."

A mile or so farther on, the Keltney Burn comes tumbling down from the heights of Schiehallion to join the Lyon. In an old Gaelic poem about the murder of James I, this burn was called the *Allt Art*, or Arthur's Burn, and east of Killin is a district known as Tirarthur, or the land of Arthur. It is said that King Arthur's journeys brought him to Tayside and presumably he dropped in on Edinburgh on his way home – King Arthur's Seat.

Higher up the Keltney Burn was Garth Castle, the impregnable lair of the Wolf of Badenoch, or the 'accursed whelp' as he was locally known. He was a natural son of Robert II, a colourful character who defied both Church and State. He burnt cathedrals, was excommunicated, did penance, was reinstated and finally buried in a very fine tomb in Dunkeld Cathedral – which can be seen to this day, whereas the tomb of St. Columba, also in Dunkeld, has disappeared from the face of the earth. He had his own private army and was uncrowned robber king of the Highlands, though latterly became something of a princely Rob Roy, plundering the rich to give to the poor.

All this time we've been on the northern side of Drummond Hill, or Druim Phinn, Fingal's Ridge, the eastern side of which was planted by Black Douglas of the trees. On the south side lies Kenmore, but we'll stop at Inchadney on the way, which is not marked on any map but was situated on the low-lying peninsula of land between Drummond Hill and the Tay. In olden days, before the fine bridge was built in 1774, Inchadney was a busy little place, for there was a vital ford here, and a ferry.

On the south side of the ford was the Inn of Muttonhole, where travellers quenched their thirst until the end of the 18th century. There were no fewer than six ferries between Kenmore and Aberfeldy, and at each there was an ale house. Whisky was forbidden to be made, or drunk, and no man was allowed more than a 'chopin' of ale if he was escorting another man's wife – a 'chopin' was a quart.

Markets were held at Inchadney till Grey Colin ordered them to be moved to Kenmore Green, and a few years later the new church was built there too, in 1579, though the old grave yard at Inchadney continued to be used – the Dean of Lismore was buried there. Eventually the third Earl of Breadalbane closed it altogether and a new one was laid out at Kenmore. It is said the grave stones were used to fill up holes made by the constant traffic of builders when Taymouth Castle was in the making. The old kirk and manse were utterly destroyed during Montrose's raid in 1645.

If you stand on the bridge that leads to Kenmore and look west you can see a little tree-covered island, close to the northern shore of the loch. This is the Isle of Loch Tay, or Sybilla's Isle; Sybilla was a queen of Scotland. When she died she was buried here in 1122. Her sorrowing husband, Alexander II, built a priory on the island so that monks might daily offer prayers for the repose of her soul, and his. This is reckoned to be an artificial island, or crannog, of which there used to be 23 others on Loch Tay, though now there are only four or five left, mainly on the south shore.

These crannogs were introduced into Scotland by the Celts, in the Iron Age, when both man and beast were predators and an island provided a measure of security. Scotland, with its island studded lochs must have been ideal terrain. But Loch Tay had no islands, hence the man-made replicas. What a labour it must have been, ferrying out all the necessary equipment, tree trunks, boulders, sods, gravel, etc., etc. The mind boggles.

There was a causeway leading from the Isle of Loch Tay to the shore. After Grey Colin had converted thc priory into a stronghold for himself, the orchard, and possibly garden, were on the loch shore. Sir Colin and his successor lived here from time to time until his great-grandson built Balloch Castle, the forerunner of Taymouth, in 1560.

When the great Montrose attacked Tayside, the Isle of Lochtay was very much involved. For Montrose himself, whose headquarters were under a pear tree in the orchard, directed the attack. The small Campbell force was soon routed but the pear tree lived on in the form of a massive table, now in the reading room at Kenmore. This was presented in 1884 by Alma, Countess of

Breadalbane and a descendant of Montrose
"as a token of the peace and love which now
unites Graham and Campbell, so long di-
vided by war and hatred."

Kenmore

N ow let's visit the inn at Kenmore.
Four hundred years ago Grey Colin
– all these early lairds of Glenorchy
were either Duncan or Colin which is, I
suppose, why they were given soubriquets
like grey, black, red, mad or hospitable.
Anyway, Grey Colin leased to his servant
Hew Hay, and his wife, the 40 penny land of
Cobble Croft, where they were to keep a
good hostelry with sufficient bread and ale in
readiness at all times to serve the people of
the district. This 'hostellarie' was to be 'loftit'
and have chimneys, doors and windows.

Crofters' homes at that time, according
to Pennant, were incredibly small and low
roofed, without any of these amenities – the
peat reek escaping through a hole in the roof.
He called them "the disgrace of North Britain, as its lakes and rivers are its glory." Yet

the inhabitants of these hovels lived to ripe old ages.

Burns once came to the inn at Kenmore and wrote his famous poem on the parlour wall above the fireplace – now protected by a sheet of glass. Not one of his better efforts in my opinion.

Once Grey Colin had ousted the Macgregors from Balloch, down near the river on the south side, he proceeded to build himself a castle there, the Isle of Lochtay not being nearly grand enough for his designs.

The village as it stands to-day was built by the third Earl. He demolished the old thatched cottages and built new ones in tidy rows north and south of the village square. The church was to the west and the entrance gates to Taymouth Castle, built by the fourth Earl at the beginning of the 19th century, on the east. This entrance is most ostentatious and quite out of keeping with the village which is otherwise attractive.

The second Marquis made further additions to Taymouth – even the name, like the edifice itself, is unpleasing. Locals, I believe, continued to call it Balloch. By the time Queen Victoria and Prince Albert paid their celebrated visit in 1842 all was complete.

But a lot happened in Kenmore before that auspicious occasion. For example in the seventeenth century, the Royal Honours of Scotland, the crown, sceptre and sword, were brought secretly to Balloch and hidden there for nine weeks while a Commonwealth army was in Scotland. Sir Robert, the tenth Laird, like most of the Campbells, was pro the establishment and would not have been suspected. It must have been a very worrying time, but in the end the honours came out of hiding, and Charles II was duly crowned King of Scotland in Scone, on January 1, 1651.

Sir Robert's grandson, who became the first Earl, did a great deal to retrieve the family fortunes, which had been decimated during the Royalist/Covenanting times.

While in London he met, wooed and won the Lady Mary Rich, well-named daughter of the Earl of Holland and a great heiress to boot. It is said he got £10,000 with her, and all in gold. Be that as it may, he sent home for a couple of stalwart ponies and two well armed Highlanders, to escort himself and his lady wife home to Scotland. When they arrived in the village square it was a strange sight to see John Campbell of Glenorchy, with his wife riding pillion, on the first pony, and the two Highlanders trotting along on either side of the second pony that was carrying the gold, and this was the way it had been all the way from London.

One Sunday morning in 1784, there were some very strange happenings in the bay just below Kenmore Bridge. The first person to notice them was the village blacksmith who had gone down to the Loch for his usual morning ablutions. The water began to ebb and flow. At one stage the bed of the bay was left dry and the river receded considerably from its usual level. These receding waters formed into a wave that rolled westwards till it met a similar wave from the opposite direction. They rose to a height of four feet when they met, and then turned towards the southern shore where they gained upon the usual high water mark by at least four feet. This went on for a long time yet all the while there was a dead calm.

Nobody knows for certain the cause of this phenomenon, but it may have had something to do with the Great Highland Fault that stretches across Scotland in a south-westerly direction. Here the earth's surface has cracked for hundreds of miles. To the south of this crack the level of the earth has sunk considerably from that on the far side and this is still going on. "Three hundred million years have not mended the scar." Earth tremors are felt at Comrie and Crieff, both on the fault.

At Fearnan the loch takes a sharp south-west turn, due to another geological fault, a small one, but sensitive to distant earth tremors. So presumably the disturbance in Loch Tay was a slight peripheral effect of some upheaval in the bowels of the earth. Now comes the climax of Kenmore's varied history. In 1842, when Queen Victoria was 23 and very much in love with Albert, they visited the Breadalbanes at Taymouth Castle. She took Scotland to her heart and loved it all her days. Never, since the time of the Stewarts, had there been such a love affair as the one that grew up between Victoria and her Scottish peoples.

She arrived one evening in September and was received by a guard of honour of Highlanders with pipes playing, guns firing and cheering crowds. It was, as she said in her diary, "as if a great chieftain in olden times was receiving his sovereign. It was princely and romantic."

That evening there was a display of fireworks, and illuminations. Forty thousand little lamps were lit in the grounds of the Castle, bonfires blazed on the hilltops, and by the light of flares and to the music of pipes, there was Highland dancing.

Albert was out shooting the next morning, while Victoria explored the grounds –

always attended by a couple of Highlanders with drawn swords. She visited the model dairy, made of quartz that sparkled in the sun, with marble floors and Dutch tiled walls and she tried her hand at making butter with a silver handled churn.

The conclusion of the visit was marked by a triumphal trip down the loch to Killin. The Queen's barge was manned by eight Highlanders and two pipers in the bows, who played and sang Highland songs for her entertainment during the journey down the loch. The Queen's barge was followed by four others, all decorated and beflagged for this great occasion.

I believe at one time it was hoped by the Breadalbanes that the Queen would buy Taymouth Castle for her Highland home, which would have helped the family coffers, but instead of Tayside she chose Balmoral and Deeside

Twenty-four years later she was to come back incognito to Taymouth and write in her diary: "I was thankful to see it again. I gazed, not without deep emotion, on the scene of our reception twenty four years ago... Albert and I were only twenty three, young and happy. How many are gone that were with us then. I was very thankful to see it again, it seemed unaltered."

But it is very altered now. The third
Marquis, just before his death, owned
400,000 acres, from Aberfeldy to the isles of
Luing and Seil on the west coast. The following appeared in *Punch* on February 4, 1903:–

From Kenmore
To Ben More,
The land is a' the Markiss's,
The mossy howes,
The heathery knowes,
An' ilka bonny park is his.

The bearded goats,
The toozie stots
And a' the braxy carcasses
Ilk crofter's rent,
Ilk tinker's tent,
An' ilka collie's bark is his.

The muircock's craw,
The piper's blaw,
The ghillies' hard day's work is his,
From Kenmore
To Ben More,
The warld is a' the Markiss's.

At the time of writing Taymouth Castle,
after passing through many hands, is leased
to an American company as a school and the

grounds form an 18 hole golf course. All their other castles are in ruins or other men's hands.

The Macnabs have returned to Kinnell, Auchmore belongs to the Hydro Board and the tenth Earl of Breadalbane lives, I believe, in Hampstead. The glory is indeed departed, but not the glory of the trees they planted; these are their best and most lasting memorial.

It's high time we left Kenmore and followed the Tay to Croftmoraig where there are some splendid specimens of standing stones – one of the most complete groups to be found in Scotland. As the Rev. Hugh McMillan says: "Uncounted centuries old, it must have been the work, not of rude savages, but of a race capable of co-operation for an end beyond their mere physical wants and who had a monumental genius."

Dull and Weem

The road from Kenmore to Aberfeldy is very beautiful; lovely old trees form an arboreal archway all along its route. But let's pretend, once more, that we've crossed the Tay on one of those six ferries of yore to visit Dull on the opposite shore. This strip of low-lying land that stretches from the eastern tip of Drummond Hill to Aberfeldy was once a continuation of Loch Tay and even now, during the winter spate, is frequently under water.

There is nothing left in Dull to show that it was once a very important place – in fact the home of learning on the mainland of Scotland – Iona, its predecessor, being of course, an island.

St. Adamnan, of Glen Lyon fame, gave instructions on his death bed that he was to be carried on his bier down the Lyon and

when the first willow ring, or 'dull', through
which the bearing sticks were placed, broke,
there he wished to be buried. His instructions
were obeyed and this was where the first
'dull' broke and Dull it has been ever since.

A church dedicated to St. Adamnan was
built here. It became an abbey, hence the
Appin of Dull as these parts are known –
Appin in the Gaelic means the district of the
Abbot. This Celtic monastery became a seat of
learning, the endowments of which were much
later transferred to Dunkeld and eventually to
St. Andrews. Dull also became a centre of the
Culdees, successors of the ancient Celtic
Church, who followed the rites and rituals of
St. Columba as opposed to Roman forms.

A few miles east of Dull, sheltering
snuggly below the Hill of Weem, is the old grey,
four-storied Menzies Castle – the ancient seat
of the clan of that name. Like other castles in
this area it was plundered by Montrose and
garrisoned by Cromwell. In more recent times
it has opened its doors to the public.

The Rock, or Hill of Weem is famous
for its caves, of which many stories have
been told. It is said that St. Cuthbert, a monk
at Melrose Abbey in the 7th century, later to
become Bishop of Lindisfarne, "was often
absent on missionary activities" in these parts
and had his cell in one of the caves. Outside

was a space of level ground and under this terrace was a narrow fissure in the rock which widened out into another cave and about this there is a strangely haunting little story. It has been turned into a Gaelic song.

The story tells how, one Sabbath day, a long, long time ago, two girls, the daughter and step-daughter of the Lady of Weem, were searching for a calf that had strayed. They followed the sound of its lowing till it brought them to the mouth of the cave. One had a bible in her hand, which protected and stayed her from entering, but the other, who had no such protection went in and was never seen alive again, though her remains were found some time later, floating by the shore of Loch Glassie, a moorland loch nearby.

The sister left outside then asked the other when she would come home and the reply was that between herself and the open air there were seven iron gates guarded by a man with a scarlet coat and she couldn't come back till the Day of Judgement. In great anguish her sister asked her yet again, and faint and far away came the answer that she would return when the time of seed-sowing and lint-pulling should coincide – or never more.

It could be a myth of purgatory, with the gentleman in the scarlet coat as the devil, but in these parts it has always been believed throughout the centuries that it had something to do with St Cuthbert. That during his frequent sojourns in this district he had fallen in love with the daughter of a neighbouring chieftain and perhaps she was having a baby and to hide his guilt he killed her.

There's another cave into which a piper went marching one fine day and never came back. But, miles away, in the direction of Rannoch Moor, you can sometimes faintly hear the sound of bagpipes that seems to be coming from the bowels of the earth. And there's a cave in which a saint once fought with the devil and came out the victor – but it couldn't have been St Cuthbert.

The old kirk of Weem – no longer in use – is very, very old, almost shrunken with age; the surrounding tombstones seem to tower over it. Hanging on a wall inside is a rusty iron collar belonging to one of the old jougs used in the punishment of clerical wrong-doers and peculiar to Scotland. This iron collar was presumably clamped round the sinner's neck and the chain attached to it was then fastened to a post or stall – rather like a form of stocks – I wonder if his fellow clerics were encouraged to pelt him with rotten eggs. In 1839 the old Kirk was handed over to Sir Nigel Menzies as a mausoleum for his family.

Now we must turn south over Wade's

Ben Lawers Hotel

Fortingall Hotel

Fortingall village

Fortingall Yew

Mains of Taymouth, Kenmore

Autumn on Loch Tay

Restored crannog, Loch Tay

Towards Glen Lyon

Taymouth Castle

Taymouth Castle gates, Kenmore

Taymouth Castle

Aberfeldy Distillery

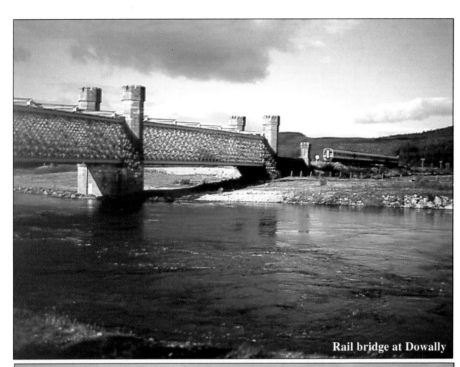

Rail bridge at Dowally

Smeaton's Bridge, Perth

most famous bridge built in 1733. It's a strong, powerful structure that has withstood all pressures from that day to this, without any re-inforcing. Perhaps it would blend more peacefully into the scenery if the general hadn't insisted on those four obelisk-like erections on the four corners of the main arch, but then perhaps that's just what he didn't want it to do. Perhaps he wanted it to be a stark reminder to the Highlanders that their day was done and that he, General Wade, had been instrumental in achieving this end – which he most certainly had. The Wordsworths didn't like it; they called it ambitious and ugly.

There is an endearing Latin inscription on the bridge that, being translated says: "Admire this military road, stretching on this side and that 250 miles beyond the limits of the Roman one, mocking moors and bogs, opened up through rocks and over mountains and, as you see, crossing the indignant Tay. This difficult work General Wade, Commander in Chief of the Forces in Scotland, accomplished by his own skill and ten years' labour of his soldiers, in the year of the Christian Era 1733."

There was a couplet in vogue at the time that went something like this:–

*"If you'd seen these roads before they
were made,
You'd lift up your hands and bless
General Wade."*

He was no Butcher Cumberland but a
decent, sensible man, as the people came to
realise after the Disarming Act of 1796, when
Highlanders were commanded to bring in
their arms. He was presented with quantities
of rusty, obsolete weapons and though he
knew full well there were dirks and broadswords a-plenty hidden in thatched roofs and
other suitable hiding places, he never made
an issue of the fact.

On the other side of the bridge the fine
cairn-like memorial to the Black Watch is to be
seen, for it was here in 1739 that the famous
Highland Regiment was founded. The forming
of these regiments was part of the plan to
channel the fighting propensities of the Highlanders into more useful activities than clan
warfare and lost causes – and it worked.

General Wade himself insisted that the
Black Watch, named after the dark colour of
their tartan compared with the English red-
coats, should be provided with clothing and
bonnets in the Highland dress. Coming from
the Commander of an Army of Occupation
this was a generous gesture and well they
repaid his generosity.

Aberfeldy

Aberfeldy is best known, I suppose, for Burns's poem 'The Birks of Aberfeldy,' in which he describes the beautiful Falls of Moness. I don't think Burns's genius was really suited to the Highlands; there are not and it seems, never have been, many 'birks', or birches, in Aberfeldy. He appears to have confused it with Abergeldie, where there are plenty.

The Falls, though, are certainly very lovely; there are three different waterfalls, the Upper, Middle and Lower all cascading down the Urlar Burn and each one is as beautiful as the other.

Beside another burn, a little to the east, the famous armourer, Andrea Ferrara, had his smithy in the sixteenth century – though what brought him to Aberfeldy from Italy I can't think. He made broadswords as renowned as any from Toledo or Damascus, and tempered them in his mountain stream. In olden times the real weapon of a Highlander was the claymore, or double handed sword, which was sometimes as long as five foot eight inches, including the handle, and needed a powerful man to wield it. Gradually this great sword was superseded by a more manageable one with a basket hilt and the old claymores were modified accordingly. But though their length was reduced, their breadth was not – and that is how many of Andrea's swords were identified: by their broad blades. His trade-mark was a St Andrews cross.

At Cluny, east of Aberfeldy, the broad strath through which the Tay has been meandering suddenly comes to an end and a great barrier of rocks forces the river downwards. The Tay thunders far below – the northern bank is called Strathtay, the southern, Grandtully, after the Stewarts of Grandtully.

Grandtully and Logierait

The old church of Grandtully, in the hamlet of Pitcairn, is very quaint, low-roofed and long since abandoned. It was built in 1533 by the Stewarts of Grandtully on the site of Adamnan's original church and restored in the 17th century. Its strangely barrel-shaped wooden roof had once been most gloriously and enthusiastically painted with strange shapes of saints and angels playing trumpets all in the gayest technicolour. Sadly these have dimmed with the dust of ages.

According, again, to the Rev. Hugh McMillan, who came here as a boy, in the mid-19th century, the body of the church had obviously been built over the graveyard of its predecessor and the floor being earthen and unpaved, if you sat in your seat and scuffled your feet there was no saying what grisly remains might come to light!

East again is Grandtully Castle, built in
1560 and now restored to its erstwhile glory by
Lady Stewart. The original castle had been on
the banks of the Tay, but the owner having
been shot outside his own front door by an
arrow from the opposite shore, it was considered advisable to build the new one in a safer
spot. It is now surrounded by lovely trees –
elms and sycamores, so that even the best of
archers could not find his mark.

Where Tummel throws in its weight with
Tay is the village of Logierait, the 'rait' part
coming from 'rath' or fortified place, more
often met in Ireland, as in Rathmore and
Rathim. There must have heen a stronghold
here defending the entrance to the valley of the
Tay. Here the Thanes of Atholl meted out
summary justice in the old Court House from
the 12th to the 18th centuries; possibly on the
site of the present inn and the old ash tree in
the garden was probably the 'hanging tree.' In
its heyday it measured 53 feet in circumference
at ground level and 40 feet three feet above
ground level. Its trunk was hollow and fitted
out as a summer house. Now, in its dotage, it is
lovingly supported by the arms of the ivy that is
slowly but surely strangling it to death.

Canada's first Liberal Prime Minister,
Alexander MacKenzie, was born in a little
thatched cottage here in Logierait.

Dunkeld

After Logierait the Tay turns south, gaining in grandeur all the way, till it reaches Dunkeld, which means 'the fort of the Culdees' who were, as we've already seen, the hierarchy of the old Celtic Church that held sway in Scotland from the dawn of Christianity to the 12th century when it gave way to Rome.

In Pictish times, from the fifth to ninth centuries, Dunkeld had the usual 'dun' situated on the hill now know as the King's Seat, where some slight remains of a building and fortifications can still be seen.

And here, in 860 Kenneth McAlpine, the first king of a united nation of Picts and Scots, brought the relics of St Columba from Iona and built a church to receive them; he made of it a seat of learning – the fount of all knowledge then was the church – and it became a second Iona to which pilgrims came from far and wide. Although Kenneth McAlpine brought these precious relics to Dunkeld for safe keeping because Iona was considered too vulnerable to Viking raids, even Dunkeld was twice attacked and once reached by these Norsemen. They brought their small, tough ponies (poor things) with them in their longships which, on landing, enabled them to make those dreaded, light-ening thrusts deep into enemy territory.

It was in the 12th century that David II laid the foundation stone of Dunkeld Cathedral and made it the seat of a Bishop and for 700 years it was the spiritual centre of Scotland, that is from 860 to 1560 when that arch icono-clast, John Knox, ordered it to be destroyed and all traces of Rome to be removed from the banks of the Tay. It was not till the Reforma-tion that it was actually made roofless, though the choir was eventually re-roofed by the Atholls and is now used as the parish church. How sad, that in such a short time, man could have destroyed the beauty of centuries of pains-taking labour and craftsmanship.

It's a particularly lovely reach of the Tay that flows through Dunkeld and makes a per-fect setting for the Cathedral with its lawns reaching to the water's edge, said to be rivalled in beauty only by Salisbury.

Telford built a bridge across the Tay, that must be getting used to such indignities by now, and though not as masterly as Wade's, it does blend beautifully with the scenery.

Where the Braan enters the Tay is the little village of Inver, whose inn must have been a welcome sight to travellers on the coach between Perth and Inverness. This was the birthplace of Scotland's most famous fiddler, Neil Gow. Raeburn painted no fewer than four portraits of him in his tartan knee-breeches with his head resting on his fiddle. The original is in the Scottish National Portrait Gallery in Edinburgh. It had been in the possession of his son, who certified that this was the painting done from life and the other three were copies.

A mile or two up the Braan valley was once a most amazing erection known as Ossian's Hall, which overhung the river just where it took an 80 foot downward plunge, causing a very fine waterfall. This building was the brainchild of a Duke of Atholl in the 18th century and very popular it proved with travellers to the Highlands. Presumably the Duke called it Ossian's Hall because his grave was said to be in Sma' Glen, not so very far away.

When Wade and his men were digging their way through the said glen, making one of their useful roads, they happened to dig it up. At least they presumed they had, for they found a twenty one foot long stone slab lying in their way and when they dug it up, thinking it might come in useful, underneath they found a stone cist, or coffin, and inside were ashes, bones, fragments of metal and some burnt heather stalks. These remains they collected and re-interred with due solemnity in a new grave, presumably beside their fine new road.

Wordsworth reckoned this was Ossian's grave too:

"In this still glen, remote from men,
Lies Ossian in the Narrow Glen."

Hence Ossian's Hall, later known as the Hermitage when the original masterpiece had been superseded by a more decorous and suitable building.

Let's return to the hall. Robert Heron, who visited in 1793, gives a vivid description. "The door was flung open and the figure of Ossian was suddenly exposed. The painting was a noble one. By Ossian we were admitted to an interior apartment, spacious, light, airy and elegant; set around with mirrors and more like a boudoir than a hermitage. This apartment hangs over the waterfall."

Evidently the walls and ceiling of this room were lined with mirrors that captured and reflected every movement of the mighty cataract as it hurled itself down the ravine, giving the impression of being actually *in* the waterfall. R. Heron was not amused and neither were the Wordsworths – I wish I'd been able to see it for myself.

South-west of Dunkeld is Birnam Hill of which the witches prophesied:

"Macbeth shall never vanquished be until Great Birnam Wood to high Dunsinane Hill Shall come against him."

Pennant in his travels once remarked that "Birnam Wood had never recovered from its arboreal march," for though it had once been a Royal Forest, even in his day it was practically bare of trees. Dunsinane lies 12 miles away to the south-east in the Sidlaw Hills. And there is, or was, an ancient hill fort there with ramparts, fosses and human bones, known locally as Macbeth's Castle. Perhaps it was.

The Tay now turns eastward on its way to meet the Isla, past Meikleour with its 600 yard beech hedge, planted at the time of Culloden. Somewhere hereabouts was Inchtuthil, originally a Pictish settlement which was taken over by the Romans and turned into a large station covering an area of 55 acres.

This was no marching camp, but one capable of wintering an army. The Romans called it Pinnata Castra, or literally, the 'feathered camp', though in this case 'feathered' referred to a particular type of rampart. Some say Inchtuthil was south of Delvine House, near Meikleour, others that it was in the triangle made by the junctions of Tay and Isla, or even that there were two Roman camps in this small area which seems highly unlikely.

It has been suggested that this was where the great battle of Mons Graupius, which gave its name to the Grampians, was fought. That there was a battle between the masters of the world, led by Agricola, and the army led by Calgacus, 'the swordsman,' is an historical fact.

In 81 A.D. Agricola led an army to the Forth-Clyde area where he built a line of forts in a vain attempt to contain the Caledonians in their mountain fastnesses. Eventually he and his legions sallied forth into Perthshire to find, if possible, and to do battle with these Caledonians, who refused to bow the knee to the might of Rome.

Tacitus, the Roman historian and Agricola's son-in-law, has told us all this but neglected to say where the battle was fought and it's been puzzling historians ever since. According to Ptolemy's map of Britain, made from information brought back by legionaries, Caledonia stretched from what is now Loch Long to the Beauly Firth, which gives plenty of choice from which to choose a site.

But, according to Tacitus, Calgacus

addressed his troops on the eve of battle and this is what Tacitus says he said. "When I reflect on the causes of war, and the circumstances of our position, I feel a strong persuasion that our united efforts this day will prove the beginning of universal liberty to Britain. For we are undebased by slavery, and there is no land behind us... Those plunderers of the world... where they make a desert they call it peace, shall not we, untouched and unsubdued and struggling not for acquisition, but for the security of liberty, show at the very first onset what men Caledonia has reserved for her defence? Be not terrified with an idle show and the glitter of gold and silver, which can neither protect nor wound... March then to battle and think of your ancestors and your posterity. ˙

This was good fighting talk, Churchillian in fact, and even if this was what Tacitus imagined Calgacus might have said (though perhaps he had a spy in the enemy camp who could write shorthand), he would never have put such fine words in to the mouth of some woad painted savage, as we are inclined to think of them.

It seems to me when historians are trying to locate the site of this battle they are neglecting a clue in the words of Calgacus "and there is no land behind us... we, at the furthest limits of land and liberty"... etc. must surely mean with their backs to the sea and there must have been a mountain nearby for the 'mons' part of it.

These requirements don't seem to be met at Inchtuthil – no sea and no mountain. Fortingall, another suggestion, doesn't appear to foot the bill either, so I go for the Beauly/ Moray Firth area, which is, I believe the latest thinking anyway, somewhere in the vicinity of Culloden, where I suppose it's just possible, though somewhat unlikely, that the Caledonians were caught with their backs to the Moray Firth, and the Grampians forming the 'mons'. That Agricola and his legions reached the Moray Firth, by way of the coast, is known; it's also known that he sent a fleet round the north of Scotland, so the legions could have been supported from the sea. But I expect Mons Graupius will keep its secret for all time.

The Romans claimed it as a victory. The enemy had disappeared and Agricola had no intention of following them into their mountain hideouts to which many, I have no doubt, had retreated on the sound assumption that a good retreat was better than a bad stand.

By now the Tay has reached its prime; there's only the Almond left to swell its banks before it flows majestically into Perth, passing close to Scone on the way.

Scone

Scone was very much at the heart of Scottish life in the old days before the joining of the crowns in 1603, for this was where her kings were crowned and here was their precious Stone of Destiny which has meant so much to them for so long.

This stone has a fascinating history – put briefly it's something like this. It was Jacob's pillow at Bethel, it came to Egypt with a prince of Athens called Gathelus who married the King of Egypt's daughter, Scota, in the time of Moses – perhaps she was the one who found him in the bullrushes.

When the plagues came to Egypt, Gathelus, Scota, their sons and the stone fled to Spain. Eventually their heirs settled in what is now Ireland, was then Scotia, whose inhabitants were the Scotti. or Scots. They brought their stone with them and for centuries the Kings of Ireland were crowned over it on the hill of Tara. From there it was brought by Fergus, the son of Erc, to Argyllshire, and placed in the Scots fortress of Dunadd, where it was used in the coronations of their kings – till it was moved to Scone.

Edward I has always been accused of pilfering and housing it at Westminster – but did he? Some say the Abbot of Scone hid the real stone when he saw the English advancing and the quarry-dressed block of red sandstone now at Westminster bears no resemblance whatever to the original, as described on the occasion of Balliol's coronation a few years earlier. Yet another unsolved mystery.

Scone Abbey was built in 1115 by Alexander II, and Knox was the cause of its downfall. In 1559, in St John's Kirk, Perth, he made another of his rabble-rousing diatribes against all things Roman, priests and so-called monuments of idolatry alike, and the mob came to Scone and did their dirty work only too well. The Abbot's palace was rebuilt and came into the possession of the future Earls of Mansfield, who built the present palace in 1803, including the gallery where Charles II was crowned in 1651. The glory of Scone has long since passed; the burial ground and the market cross, both enclosed within the palace walls, are all that is left of bygone days.

Perth

Ａnd so to Perth, where our journey
ends. The sad thing about Perth is
that, though it was such an impor-
tant town in Scottish history, all its ancient,
historic buildings have been pulled down –
mainly in the 19th century.

Its original name was 'Aber-ta' or the
mouth of the river, for, as we saw in the
beginning, the old British word 'ta', possibly
pronounced taa as in Tay, means the river, so
when we talk of the Tay we're really calling it
the river, which sounds complicated but
makes sense. Aber-ta became Bertha and
finally Perth – I believe B and P are inter-
changeable in Gaelic.

According to Richard of Cirencester,
Perth was built by Agricola during his cam-
paign in the year 82 on the site of an old
British town dating from pre-Christian times,
with a temple dedicated to Mars. Agricola is

said to have worshipped at this altar, presumably praying for a successful outcome to his efforts at curbing the barbarians. Though he was officially, I believe, a Christian, it's true that old habits die hard.

Perth was the capital of the kingdom, the usual seat of its sovereigns and High Courts of Justice. Edward I, the 'hammer of the Scots', was forever visiting it, demanding homage from all and sundry. It was on his last visit that he went off with the Stone of Destiny and burnt "all the Chronicles of the Scottish Nation... to the end that the memorie of the Scots should perish."

Wallace reconquered Perth from the English on two occasions; he even crossed the border and created havoc as far south as Newcastle. He was finally betrayed, captured and tried as a traitor at Westminster; his end was cruel – hanged, disembowelled while still alive, and quartered. The quarters were sent to Berwick, Newcastle, Stirling and Perth to be shown to the people – Perth received his right leg.

Edward III committed fratricide on the high altar of St John's Church. James I was assasinated at the Blackfriars Monastery, the various forms of torture suffered by the regicides before they were allowed to die are really too horrible to relate – they put

Wallace's treatment in the shade. But for sheer cold-blooded, calculated slaughter, the Battle of the Clans or the 'Threttie against Threttie' is in a class of its own.

This was fought on the North Inch, beside the Tay. The contestants were the Clans Chattan and Kay who were at perpetual warfare with each other, and robbed and plundered the entire neighbourhood. A plan was thought of to put an end to these menaces to society, which was agreed to by the respective chiefs, namely, that thirty of the best warriors from each side would meet on the North Inch, armed with broadsword and axe, and fight it out to the finish.

An enormous crowd, including King Robert III and his court, gathered to watch the sport. The ensuing carnage was horrible; heads were cloven asunder, limbs were lopped from the trunk, the meadow drenched with blood and covered with dead and wounded men. At the end of it all one man from Clan Kay survived to swim the Tay, because the eleven Clan Chattan men were quite incapable of stopping him. The result of this slaughter was – just what had been hoped for – there was peace in the land for a while. But nobody knows to this day to what clans Kay and Chattan belonged – no Highland family claims them.

In 1651 Cromwell erected on the South Inch what must rank as the most short-lived fortress ever built. To get the necessary stones he knocked down all the surrounding buildings, including the hospital built by James I and the Greyfriars Monastery. Charles II gave it back to the people of Perth in recompense for their losses incurred during its building, and soon it was as though it had never been

Here we must leave the Tay, that great river that has seen so much of, and done so much for, Scotland's story. Leave it to find its own way to the open sea, in the comforting knowledge that, though kings may come and go and kingdoms rise and fall, as long as the rain comes down from heaven and that little spring rises in the corrie on the Ben of the Calves, the Tay will still be there, like Tennyson's brook, for ever and ever.

Amen.

FURTHER READING

In Famed Breadalbane
  The Rev. William A Gillies
Fair Perthshire
  Hamish Miles
The Highland Tay
  The Rev. Hugh Macmillan
In the Hills of Breadalbane
  VA Firsoff
Historic Scenes of Perthshire
  William Marshall
The Lairds and Lands of Lochtayside
  John Christie
The Central Highlands
  Ian Finlay
The Massacre of Glencoe and the Campbells of Glen Lyon
  The Rev. George Gilfillan
Four Hundred Years Around Kenmore
  Duncan Fraser